Walt Disney
Bambi's Snowy Day

Written by Betty Birney

Illustrated by David Pacheco
and Diana Wakeman

A GOLDEN BOOK • NEW YORK

Western Publishing Company, Inc., Racine, Wisconsin 53404

One cold and frosty morning, Bambi woke up and could not believe his eyes! Overnight, everything in the forest had turned white!

Plop! A clump of snow dropped onto Bambi's head. He shook his head, trying to figure out what it was.

"It's snow," said Thumper as he hopped toward Bambi. "That means it's winter. Let's go and play!"

"Okay," answered Bambi excitedly. "And we'll get Flower, too."

"Now you two be careful," cautioned Bambi's mother. "Don't get lost."

"We promise to be careful!" said Bambi and Thumper as they hurried off into the forest.

"Look, Bambi," said Thumper as he glanced back at their path in the snow. "We'll be able to follow our footprints home."

As Bambi and Thumper romped around in the woods, they noticed another set of footprints in the fluffy white snow.

"Those aren't *my* footprints. And they aren't *your* footprints," said Thumper. "Hey, maybe they're Flower's footprints!"

"Let's follow them and find out," suggested Bambi.
So Bambi and Thumper followed the new set of footprints.
They wove in and out among the trees.

They followed the trail of footprints until it ended at the base of a hollow tree.

"Flower's den must be in here," said Thumper.

But instead of Flower, Bambi and Thumper found a family of opossums. "Hello, Opossums!" they called.

The young deer leaned into the hollow. "It's me—Bambi!" he shouted.

"And me—Thumper," added the little rabbit, thumping his hind foot.

The opossums came outside to say hello.

Bambi explained that he and Thumper were looking for Flower. "We thought we were following *his* footprints, but we found *you* instead!"

"Look! Here are some more footprints," shouted a young opossum. "*These* probably belong to Flower. I'll go with you and we'll find him in no time!"

The new footprints were much smaller than the first set.

"This is fun!" shouted Thumper. "These footprints hop all over the place, just like me!"

The three friends happily bounded along the zigzagging path until they almost hit their noses on a snow-covered tree stump. The footprints had disappeared!

The three friends looked around. There, on top of the stump,
sat a red cardinal.

"Hello," said Thumper to the cardinal. "Have you seen Flower?"
But the cardinal just shook his head.

Then the cardinal chirped and hopped over to the other side of the stump. He was trying to show them something.

"Look!" shouted Thumper. "Here are more footprints! Maybe *these* belong to Flower. Come on, everybody!"

Thumper led Bambi, the opossum, and the cardinal along the new trail of footprints to the top of a hill. Suddenly Thumper vanished from sight.

"Where did he go?" wondered Bambi as he scrambled to the top of the hill. Below him, Bambi saw Thumper *standing* on the pond. He couldn't believe his eyes!

"It's all right!" shouted Thumper. "The water's stiff." The little rabbit slid across the ice and did a twirl. "Come on, everybody. This is great!"

Just then, Bambi slipped on the snow and tumbled all the way
down the hill, landing on the slick ice.

"Whee!" giggled Bambi as he slid across the pond's surface.

Soon the opossum and cardinal joined Bambi and Thumper
on the ice.

It didn't take long for Thumper to teach his friends how to ice-skate.

"It's easy!" he told Bambi. "Just slide."

Bambi didn't think that skating was easy. But he did think that it was lots of fun.

Suddenly the little red cardinal began to chirp again.
"Maybe he's found more footprints!" suggested the opossum.
He had indeed. So Bambi and his friends set off again to
find Flower.

First the new trail led to a narrow stream that was almost
hidden in the snow. Then the footprints circled around the
stream and brought them to another hollow tree.

"Maybe we'll find Flower here," said Bambi.

The animals peeked into the hollow tree. But instead of Flower, they found a family of raccoons eating their breakfast.
"Have you seen Flower?" Bambi asked.

The raccoons shook their heads. "I never saw a flower in the snow before," answered one raccoon. "But we will help you look for one."

The friends went outside to search for more footprints in the snow.

Then suddenly Friend Owl swooped down from the trees. "What's the commotion?" he asked. "Where are you going?"

"We're looking for Flower," explained Bambi.

"But every time we follow his footprints, they turn out to belong to somebody else," added Thumper.

Friend Owl chuckled. "You won't find Flower's footprints in the snow now. He's hibernating."

"Hibernating? What's that?" asked Bambi.

"Follow me," said Friend Owl.

He led Bambi and his friends through the snow over rocks and stream and fallen trees. Pretty soon they reached a hole at the side of a hill. It was very quiet all around. Then they heard a familiar soft snoring coming out of the opening.

The animals peered into the cozy den. There they saw Flower.
He was all snuggled up on a soft cushion of leaves and twigs,
sound asleep.

"Wake up! Wake up!" shouted Bambi and Thumper.

Flower opened one eye and yawned a big yawn.

"Is it spring yet?" he asked.

"No," said Bambi. "Winter is just beginning."

Flower yawned again, even more broadly. "Well, good night then," he said. He pulled his warm, fluffy tail over himself like a blanket and was soon fast asleep.

"*That's* hibernating," Friend Owl explained. "He'll sleep until spring."

Suddenly the raccoons and the opossum began to yawn.

"That sounds like a very good idea," said the opossum. He and the raccoons wandered off home to catch a long winter's nap.

Bambi felt a little sad. "I'm going to miss our new friends," he said to Thumper.

"Me too," said Thumper. Then he thought of something. "I know. We can go and play with all my brothers and sisters!"

"That's a great idea!" exclaimed Bambi.

The two friends soon found the rest of Thumper's family, and they all had lots of wonderful winter adventures together!